To my friend and sister, Gail Fay Scho, with love.

Dad taught me the joy of listening to tales,

you taught me the joy of telling them.

V.S.C.

THE
DEVIL
&
MOTHER
CRUMP

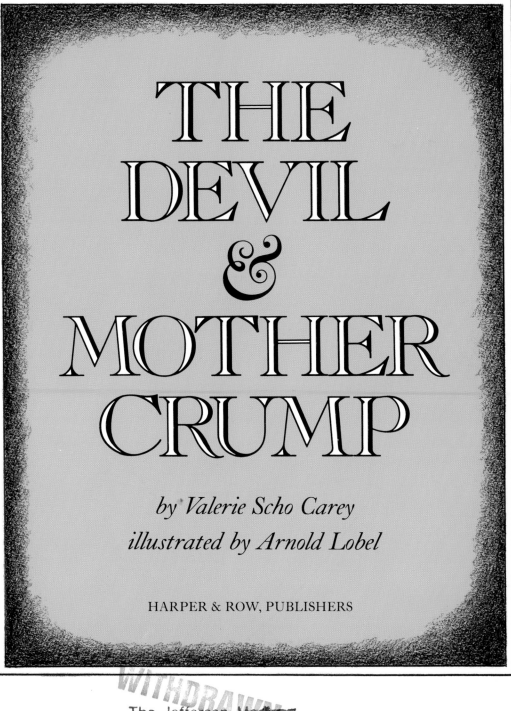

THE DEVIL & MOTHER CRUMP

by Valerie Scho Carey

illustrated by Arnold Lobel

HARPER & ROW, PUBLISHERS

The Devil & Mother Crump
Text copyright © 1987 by Valerie Scho Carey
Illustrations copyright © 1987 by Arnold Lobel
All rights reserved. No part of this book may be
used or reproduced in any manner whatsoever without
written permission except in the case of brief quotations
embodied in critical articles and reviews. Printed in
the United States of America. For information address
Harper & Row Junior Books, 10 East 53rd Street,
New York, N.Y. 10022. Published simultaneously in
Canada by Fitzhenry & Whiteside Limited, Toronto.
10 9 8 7 6 5 4 3 2 1
First Edition

Library of Congress Cataloging-in-Publication Data
Carey, Valerie Scho.
    The Devil & Mother Crump.

    Summary: The Devil meets his match in a feisty old
baker woman who tricks him into granting her three
very strange wishes.
    [1. Devil—Fiction.   2. Bakers and bakeries—
Fiction]   I. Lobel, Arnold, ill.   II. Title.
PZ7.C21434De 1987   [E]   87-64
ISBN 0-06-020982-8
ISBN 0-06-020983-6 (lib. bdg.)

Once there was a baker woman by the name of Mother Crump. She was such a stingy and mean lot that her husband and children ran away from home just to get shut of her. Mother Crump never gave anything to anyone unless she expected something back. That's a fact. Folks around here will tell you how once a young fellow, a stranger to these parts, was passing by Mother Crump's bake shop. He smelled the good smell of baking bread, and it made his mouth water. Thinking it might be getting near to lunch, he leaned in through the open door and asked Mother Crump for the time. She eyed him once over, saw the money purse tied about his waist, and figured he must know that she'd expect to be paid for giving him the time. "Eleven o'clock," she said, holding out her hand for her money.

"Thank you, ma'am. I'll be back for some of that bread real soon." And the young man pecked the brim of his hat with one finger, gave her a big smile, and stepped out on his way down the street.

Well, Mother Crump was so angry she ran out of her shop and grabbed hold of the young man. She snatched back the time she'd just given him, and she pulled so hard that a goodly number of the young man's years came away in her hands. She left him there, turned back into a squalling babe in diapers. That's how mean Mother Crump was.

Of course, anyone as mean as Mother Crump is bound to set folks talking. "Mean as the Devil," said some. "Meaner than the Devil," said others. Some of that talk reached clear on down to Lucifer, the very Devil, and it made him mighty curious. He decided to pay Mother Crump a visit to see for himself.

Not long afterward, while Mother Crump was sweeping out the bake oven, an old man knocked on

her door and poked his cracked and crinkled face into her kitchen. "Good woman," he said, "I've traveled a long road, and I'm feeling mighty weak. Would you please be so kind as to direct me to the nearest inn where I might get some food and a bed for the night?"

Mother Crump looked the old man up and down. That didn't take long because he wasn't very tall. His clothes were old-fashioned and stained with road dust, but they were made of rich red velvet. His boots were made out of red leather, with big, shiny silver buckles. His eyes glowed like coals, and when Mother Crump looked into them she saw no reflections. But his purse was full, and that was what mattered.

"Look-a-now," she said. "If you can pay, you're welcome to spend the night right here." And she punched the broom handle at him on the word "pay."

"I always see that those who deal with me get what they're owed," said the old man.

Early the next morning, when Mother Crump got up

to sweep the ashes from the fire, she saw that the old man's bed was empty. "He's skipped out without payin'!" she bellowed. "If I ever set eyes on that good-for-nothin' again, I'll whup his hide."

As she was muttering and cursing, a fine-looking young man came to the door. "Good morning," he said, sweeping the hat from his head.

"Go away!" snapped Mother Crump. "I've had my bellyful of strangers this mornin'."

"But I was hoping," said the young man, "that you might have a room I could let."

Mother Crump looked at the young man's splendid coat and ruffled neckcloth. Then she looked at his eyes and saw that they glowed but held no reflections.

"You!" she exploded. "Thought you could trick me out of another night's lodging with your disguises, did you? Well, once lucky, twice a fool. Pay up!" she barked, and catching him off guard, she yanked him inside the shop.

Mother Crump reached for her bread peel. She swung it at Lucifer, but he skipped out of the way. Again she swung, again and again, until she had him backed up against the hearth.

Once more she let that bread peel fly, and Lucifer leaped backward, falling right smack onto the hearth. A cloud of black soot spumed into the air. His fine clothes were ruined. His face was smeared with soot. When Mother Crump raised that peel up to crack it down on his head, he'd had enough. "I'll pay!" he wailed.

Mother Crump lowered the peel to rest just inches above his head.

"Now you're talkin'," she said.

"I'll give you three wishes," said Lucifer. "Anything you want."

"My money!" she shouted, and swung the peel high for another whack at him; but his strange, glowing eyes looked up at her, and she checked her swing. "There's

somethin' mighty peculiar about this fellow," she thought.

"All right," she said, "I'll take the wishes. But I warn you, you'd better make good."

"I told you before," hissed Lucifer. "Those who deal with me get what they're owed."

"First, I want you to make it so as anyone who so much as peeks into my flour barrel will be clapped inside and have to stay there till I wish 'em out. Understand?" Mother Crump glared at the Devil. "Second, I want anyone who messes with my bread dough to be stuck fast to it till I set 'em free." Again she glared at him, and he glared back. "And third, anyone who dares poke around the birch tree in my yard will be tangled tight in its branches and not get free till I let 'em go."

Lucifer arched his eyebrows and clacked his tongue. "Are you sure you wouldn't rather have a pot of gold or a magic bowl that never runs out of dough or a bake

oven that will never burn bread?"

"No!" said Mother Crump. "And if you don't want to be whupped up the side of your head with this bread peel, you'll pay me what I ask."

"Then that's what you've got. Now help me up."

"Help yourself," said Mother Crump.

That was the final insult. Lucifer pulled himself up and brushed the soot from his coat. "You may not know who you're talking to now," he growled, "but you'll find out when Death comes calling. Then it's *I* who'll have the last word." With that, he shot straight up the chimney. But one boot caught on the bricks and flew off, giving Mother Crump just an eye wink full of one cloven hoof.

"Now ain't that somethin'. That there was the Devil himself I beat!" And she picked up the boot, spat on it and rubbed it so it shined real pretty, and set it up on her mantel. After that she was so puffed full of pridefulness that she grew meaner than ever.

Years passed, and finally Death did come to call on Mother Crump. "Come along, Mother Crump," he said. "It's time."

"Well, I'm not ready. I've got bread to bake," she barked, and she whacked him hard with her peel.

Now Death knew what had happened to Lucifer when he'd come up against this woman, and he wasn't about to let himself in for a similar beating. "Well," declared Death, "if you won't come peaceable-like, then the Devil can take you himself!" And he backed out the door. Mother Crump snorted and kicked the door shut after him.

Death was hopping mad, and he went straight to Lucifer.

"Don't you worry," said Lucifer, his wicked eyes narrowing to slits. "I'll take care of Mother Crump."

But Lucifer remembered his last meeting with Mother Crump. So just to keep a safe distance, he sent one of his little devils after her.

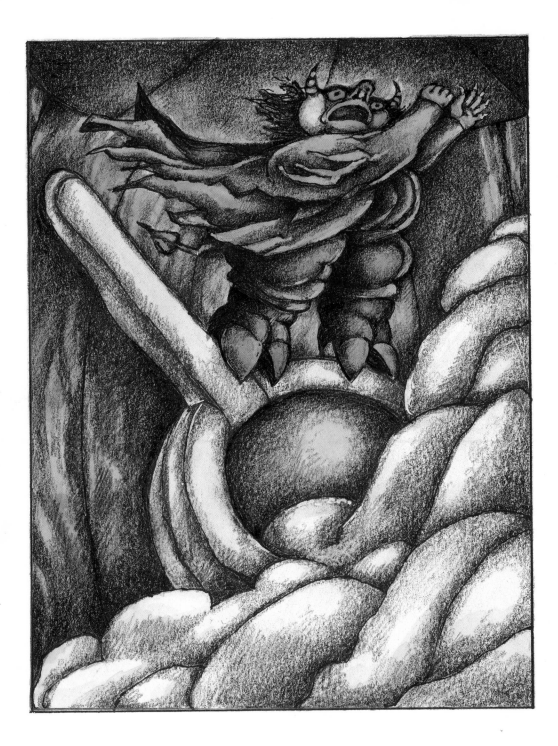

She was scooping flour from a barrel when the little devil arrived. "Let's go, Mother Crump. Lucifer is ready for you."

Mother Crump looked that little devil in the eye and said, "I'll come. But only after I get this bread baked. If you'd reach down inside this barrel and scoop out some flour it'd sure speed things along." Mother Crump lifted off the lid. "You're such a little devil, and it's a deep barrel, so I suspect you'll have to climb inside."

The little devil jumped into the barrel, and just as he did, Mother Crump clapped the lid on tight.

"Hey! Let me outta here!" screeched the little devil.

Mother Crump just reached out kind of casual-like, snapped a splinter of wood off the lid, and commenced to picking at her teeth.

The little devil started rattling and thumping at the lid, but it held firm. "Let me outta here!"

"I guess I'll have to make do without that flour," said Mother Crump, picking up her mixing spoon.

Now that little devil was really provoked. He began leaping around inside the barrel so that it pitched and swayed from side to side, till it fell right over and rolled around the kitchen. He knocked over the chair and stools, spilled the butter from the churn, and scattered pots, pans, and kettles all over the place.

"Let me out!" moaned the devil, his breath just about gone. "Let me out and I'll go home and never trouble you again!"

"That sounds fair to me," said Mother Crump, "providin' you get this kitchen cleaned up before you go."

"Anything," whined the little devil. "Just let me out."

So she set him free, and he cleaned up the kitchen and then lit on out of Mother Crump's place so fast that his feet never touched the ground.

Some time later, Mother Crump was kneading her dough when she heard the clickety-clack of hooves on the wooden floor. She looked up, and there across the

table from her stood a second little devil, just a scratch bigger than the first.

"Come on, Mother Crump," said the devil. "Lucifer wants me to fetch you down to Hell, and I mean to be quick about it."

"Well, I can't go," said Mother Crump. "Not till I've finished punchin' down this dough." And back to work she went, at a nice easy pace that just set that little devil's teeth on edge.

"You're too slow," he said, shoving her aside. "Let me in there and I'll get this done."

So that devil, he punched one fist into that dough, and it stuck fast. He punched in the other fist, and it stuck too. Then he stomped on the dough with his right foot, and it got stuck. So he stomped in with his left foot, and sure enough it stuck too. He started to rocking back and forth, and soon he fell over and started to roll around on the floor. He rolled around and around, wrestling with that dough till he was all mixed up with

it. It wasn't long till he looked like nothing more than a great lump of dough with two eyes and a tail. "You're doin' a fine job," crowed Mother Crump.

"Helphh!" came the muffled cry from out of the dough ball. "Gemme outta heah!"

"Do you promise to go away and leave me be?" said Mother Crump.

The ball of dough grunted and rocked up and down and sideways.

"Then be free!" she said.

That little devil bolted for home so fast he left scorch marks on the path.

Two days passed, and on the morning of the third, while Mother Crump was setting her loaves in the oven, a dark shadow poured into the room, pushing out the light and filling the place with a deep kind of darkness. Mother Crump twisted her head around to look back over her shoulder at the open door. At first she could barely see because the room had grown so dark. Then the figure in the doorway took shape and commenced to glowing red around the edges like coals in a fire.

"Mother Crump," said Lucifer, in a steely voice that made her bones shiver, "I've come to take you down to Hell."

Now Mother Crump took notice. This wasn't some half-growed goblin she was dealing with. This was Lucifer himself, and it was plain that he was real angry. But she wasn't about to give in. No, sir. She liked a good tussle. "Old goat-foot," she said. "Who do you think you are, ordering me about in my own place? I've bread to bake, so you'd best clear out or I'll take a birch switch to you!" And she set back to work shoveling her loaves into the heated oven.

Lucifer snarled. "We'll just see who gets the whipping this time!" And he whirled himself about and marched straight for the birch tree in the yard. He was so wrought up that he forgot all about that third wish he'd granted many years before.

He reached up and broke off a switch. But before he could pull it down, the branches caught hold of him, scooped him up into the center of the tree, and held him fast, scratching his face, tangling in his tail, and twisting around his neck so as to choke the breath out of him.

"Let me go," he rasped. His face was pretty near blue, but the harder he thrashed, the tighter the tree held him.

Mother Crump came running to see what the ruckus was about, though she had a pretty good idea of what she'd find.

"Get me down from here!" pleaded Lucifer.

"Swear that you'll go away and that neither you nor your kin will ever bother me again, and I'll let you go," said Mother Crump.

"I swear it," he gasped.

"Well then, be free!" And Lucifer fell out of the tree, landing with a thump. He picked himself up and ran off so fast that the dust didn't have a chance to kick up under his feet.

Mother Crump slapped her sides and doubled over laughing. "Now aren't I one fine lady, outsmartin' all those devils?" And she went back inside to get on with her baking.

The years went by. Mother Crump got old and then older. Finally she was too worn out to live anymore, and so she just lay down and died. But that wasn't the end of Mother Crump's story. No, sir. Her soul packed up her bags and bread peel and climbed up to Heaven, but Heaven wouldn't have her. So she slid on down to Hell. When Lucifer and his little devils saw her coming, he ran to lock the gate. "Get out of here!" he hollered, nearly frantic. "We want no more trouble with you, Mother Crump."

"I won't get," said Mother Crump, who was just as ornery as ever. "I've no place else to go." She plunked down her bags and sat down to wait till those devils

came to their senses and let her in.

Lucifer twisted his tail nervously. "What are you waiting for?" he asked. "Get going." He shook his fist at her, but Mother Crump could see that he had the jitters, and she'd had enough of this lollygaggin', so she picked up her bread peel, sauntered up to the gate, and commenced to whacking away at the lock.

"If you won't open up, I'll bust my way in," she puffed as she swung the peel. The gate rattled, and the lock began to bend.

"Stop! Wait!" shouted Lucifer. He reached round and picked up a red-hot coal. "Take this," he said, shoving the coal through the bars at Mother Crump. "You're just mean enough to go start a Hell of your own. Now go away, and never come back!"

Mother Crump dropped the coal into one of her bags. "Well, I never cared much for the thought of your company either," she snorted, and with a satisfied laugh she set on her way back up to Heaven. When she got

there she chucked that bag of hers with the Devil's coal in it right over the gate.

The angels took one look at that smoking bag that came plunking down among them, and right away they knew what was inside. Not a one of them would go near it to pitch it back. Finally one called out, "Mother Crump, come here and fetch this bag of yours. It's not fitting for it to be in Heaven."

So the angel opened the gate for Mother Crump, and she strolled right in, picked up her bag, and looked around. "You know," she said, "I like it here." And after that there was no getting Mother Crump to leave. She built herself a bake oven right there in the clouds. She's still there. On warm summer nights you can see the glow of her fire in the sky. Folks call it "heat lightning." And way in the distance you may hear her banging and rattling her pots and pans. The noise sounds an awful lot like thunder.